INDIA-THE OTHER SIDE

WHY IS LIFE PATHETIC IN INDIA-MY OBSERVATIONS AND EXPERIENCES

ALPHONSE AMALRAJ VISWASAM
PHD.

Made with ♥ on the Notion Press Platform
www.notionpress.com

Contents

Preface

India is seen by all other nations as a most populated, diverse (in race, caste, language, culture, customs, food, climate, etc), technologically advanced (as in space research), economically powerful, religious, democratic country. According to the World GDP Ranking 2024 list, India is the fifth largest economy in the world. The latest annual report (2024) by Global Firepower (GFP) revealed that India has maintained its position as the world's fourth largest military power. But then why do the younger generation wish to emigrate abroad to study, work and settle there. During the past 150 years, more than 100 million people have migrated for work. And since 2011, over 1.6 million people have relinquished their Indian citizenship leading to loss of billions in tax revenue for India. Why do many of the tourists visiting the tourist spots in India (specially in North) have given a negative review (such as insecurity, cheating, harassment, polluted environment and poverty.

Though many blame colonialism under British rule as a reason for the poverty and pitiable state. They fail to see the good side - how the divided nation was united for freedom, how the education, infrastructure such as the road-rail network, industries, and communication systems were improved. Superstitious customs as 'Sati', child sacrifice, child marriage were abolished. During my official visit as a guest of the US government, people used to ask about ground situations. They remarked if the stray dogs, cattle roam the dirty streets freely and cows are worshipped?

Whatever information I have documented in this book are my own observations and experiences during my last 50 years. These facts are not limited to the place or region where I lived. I have travelled extensively around the length and breadth of the country and also around the world. Spent considerable time in Canada and the USA. I have lived for 10 years in Rajasthan and another 15 years in Kerala and the rest in the southern state of Tamil nadu. As a genetic resources research scientist, I conducted many explorations to collect crops and wild plants, travelling extensively in Kerala, Tamil nadu, Karnataka (in south), Gujarat, Rajasthan (in west), Uttarakhand (in north), West Bengal, Tripura, Meghalaya, Manipur, Nagaland (in east). I also visited limited areas or places in Kashmir, Bihar, Assam, Andhra and Andaman Islands in Bay of Bengal.

Hence in this publication, the ground realities are given - the negative aspects of the 'dark side' which has greatly influenced and affected me. Why is life not happy and contented in India in spite of scientific and economic advancements ? I used to wonder: 'Can India ever reach the status of present-day China?' No wonder India is ranked 126th out of 143 nations in the World Happiness Report recently released on March 20, 2024, the UN's International Day of Happiness. India is ranked behind countries such as Libya, Iraq, Palestine, and Niger, according to the findings. This book explores why for an average common man life is not happy here in India, listing the possible reasons for the present pathetic, pitiable and deplorable state.

CHAPTER I

Introduction

"We owe a lot to the Indians, who taught us how to count, without which no worthwhile scientific discovery could have been made." – Albert Einstein

India, a nation with extremes like extremely rich and extremely poor; a nation of great Economic power but with poor economic condition of the common man; a country with many languages, races, castes, as well as gods. Both beautiful, clean cities or tourist spots as well as very dirty polluted towns or areas and villages with poor infrastructure. High rise buildings/apartments or large, posh houses and slums in the same cities (example Mumbai). Geographically, snow in the north, desert with almost no rainfall on the western side (Rajasthan desert with rainfall of only 100 mm/year) and tropical evergreen forest in the south and east, and heaviest rainfall (wettest place Mawsynram with 11,875 mm/year precipitation) on the eastern part.

In the eyes of the advanced western world, India is seen as a most populated, diverse (in race, caste, language, culture, customs, food, climate, etc), technologically advanced (as in space research), economically powerful, religious, democratic country. According to the World GDP Ranking 2024 list, India is the fifth largest economy in the world. The latest annual report (2024) by Global Firepower (GFP) revealed that India has maintained its position as the world's fourth largest military power. The literacy rate is about 76% as compared to China with 99%.

But then, why do the younger generation wish to emigrate abroad to study, work and settle there. During the past 150 years, more than 100 million people have migrated for work. And since 2011, over 1.6 million people have relinquished their Indian citizenship leading to loss of billions in tax revenue for India. Why do many of the tourists visiting the tourist spots in India (specially in North) have given a negative review of their visit (such as insecurity, cheating, harassment, polluted environment and poverty. Though many blame colonialism under British rule as a reason for the poverty and pitiable state. They fail to see the good side - how the divided nation was united for freedom, how the education, infrastructure such as the road-rail network, industries, and communication systems were improved. Superstitious customs as 'Sati', child sacrifice, child marriage were abolished.

India had a glorious past from the time of Harappa civilization (2,500 BC) and settlement to Aryan invasion. One of the oldest religions, the Hindu religion that has been followed from the Harappa times and even at the time when Aryans invaded India. Later, in the Fifth century, Buddhism and Jainism arose, and later Sikhism also. All religions in India were influenced by each other, but it was Jainism and Buddhism that mainly brought non-violence and vegetarian aspects into Indian religions.

Recently many books on the backward and pathetic condition of India (its governance, bureaucracy and people) have been published. Nobel laureate Naipaul V.S. had published two books on India; '**AnArea of Darkness**' in 1964, an semi-autobiographical account on the 'dark' side of India and '**A Wounded Civilisation**' in 1975 which casts a more analytical eye than before over Indian attitudes. The recent book '**The Less Sparkled Dark Side of India**' authored by Senthilkumar (2021), deals with the drawbacks of India. 'Being democratic and having millions of masterminds, India isn't a developed country still. This has to be taken into serious discussion,' states the author. Daksh Tyagi (2019) in his book '**A Nation of Idiots**' is very critical of our nature, culture and customs. The famed Punjabi author Khushwant Singh (2003) in his book, '**The End of India**' forces us to 'confront the absolute corruption of religion that has made us among the most brutal people on earth. And communal politics is only the most visible of the demons we have nurtured and let loose upon ourselves'.

CHAPTER II

Early History

History

People all around the world are fascinated by the ancient Indian history, culture and the way people are still connected with their roots. India can claim to be one of the world's oldest civilisations. India's written history can be traced back to the Vedas. As a result, writing a book on Indian history that covers the subject in its entirety may seem impossible. Many kings have had an impact on Indian history. Many queens, countless empires, religions, and, finally, its people shaped it. Unsurprisingly, thousands of academic and popular books have been written about India's history. As a result, finding books on this ancient civilisation and its history can be challenging.

Anthropology

In his book '**The Wonder That Was India**', Basham A.L., states: "It appears that some of the Harappans were people of the long-headed, narrow-nosed, slender Mediterranean type found all over the ancient Middle East and in Egypt and forming an important element of the Indian population at the present day.

~ A second element was the Proto-Australoid, with flat nose and thick lips, related to the Australian aborigines and to some of the wild hill-tribes of modern India.

~ A single skull of Mongolian type has been found and one of the short headed Alpine type.

All we can say with certainty is that the inhabitants of the Indus cities were of a type widely found further to the west, and that their descendents must survive in the present-day population of

India. The Indian is usually a blend of Mediterranean and Proto-Australoid, the two chief ethnic factors in the Harappa culture. Moreover, the Harappa religion seems to show many similarities with those elements of Hinduism which are especially popular in the Dravidian country.

Aryans migrants settle in the north

Five thousand years ago, cities like Harappa and Mohenjo-Daro thrived in the Indus Valley. They were inhabited by Dravidians, indigenous Indians. However, around four thousand years ago, the Indus Valley Civilization was in decline, and a new people, the Aryans, moved in. Aryan peoples are a diverse collection of Indo-European peoples speaking Indo-Aryan languages migrated into the Indian subcontinent, driving the original Dravidians to the south. Historically, Aryans were the Indo-Iranian speaking pastoralists who migrated from Central Asia into South Asia and introduced the Proto-Indo-Aryan language

The Dravidians driven to the south

•Some experts claim that the Harappa folk were Dravidians and say their language was a very primitive form of Tamil.

•It is suggested that the Harappa people consisted of a Proto-Australoid element, which in time covered the whole of India, overlaid by a Mediterranean one, which entered India at a very early period, bringing with it the elements of civilisation.

•Under the pressure of further invasions, this Mediterranean element spread throughout the sub-continent, and, again mixing with the indigenous peoples, formed the Dravidians.

•A recent theory holds that the Dravidians came to India from the west by sea as late as the second half of the 1st millennium B.C.

CHAPTER III

'A Wounded Civilization'

Invasions and Colonialism

For centuries, India has been a region for every possible invasion by outsiders denuding it of its economic and cultural wealth. After the invasion of the mighty warrior-like Aryan race from Central Asia, later Mughal kings from the Middle East, then came the colonisation of the British Empire. Although the people suffered during this British rule, there were many 'plus points.' All the people, in spite of different languages, religions, castes, became united to fight against the rule. With diverse languages, English language united all literate Indians, helping to travel or emigrate abroad. The basic infrastructure of the country was developed, such as roads, transport, railway lines, telegraph network, etc. Industries and factories were established with modern machinery providing jobs to the working class.

Emergence of the Elite

One of the major effects of Colonialism was the emergence of Indian bourgeoisie who appropriated a lot of money with the connivance of the British rulers. Their gross profit especially during the world war period was huge. Offshoot was the trend towards landlordism. They fleeced the poor peasants without any conscience. The western style of life and capitalist philosophy took deep roots into the upper class elite. On the fact that the Indian Bourgeoisie making huge profit at the expense of the poor, S. Kappan (1982) in his publications, **'Cultural and Class domination'** and **'Socialist perspectives'** stated, 'it is not those who make cars that travel in them. It is not those who till the soil who eat its produce or those who make nice garments go about clad in rags. Those who build mansions are condemned to live in slums and so on'. Much of the industrial wealth and business are accumulated by a few top Millionaires or Billionaires (like Adanis, Ambanis, Tatas, Birlas, etc).

'A Wounded Civilization'

Indian origin Naipaul V.S. who lived in Trinidad and London has published 30 books and is winner of the Nobel Prize (2001) for Literature. The second book in V. S. Naipaul's acclaimed Indian trilogy: in 1964, he published '**An Area of Darkness**', his semi-autobiographical account of a year in India. Two visits later, prompted by the Emergency of 1975, he came to write India: '**A Wounded Civilization**'. In this work he casts a more analytical eye than before over Indian attitudes, while recapitulating and further probing the feelings aroused in him by this vast, mysterious, and agonised country. According to V.S.Naipaul (1979) in his book 'India-a wounded civilization', said," The crisis of India is not only political or economic. The larger crisis is of a wounded old civilization that has at last become aware of its inadequacies and is without the intellectual means to move ahead" What he saw and heard – evoked so superbly and vividly in these pages – reinforced in him a conviction that India, wounded by a thousand years of foreign rule, has not yet found an ideology of regeneration. A work of fierce candour and precision, it is also a generous description of one man's complicated relationship with the country of his ancestors. In his book '**Western media narratives on India:** From Gandhi to Modi', Umesh Upadhyay states, 'The Western media's approach to India shows how the English press continues to perpetuate the West's long-held prejudices against India. With time, these attacks have intensified, particularly on a resurgent India. He accuses the western media that the negative aspects are solely focussed.

CHAPTER IV

Culture, Socialism and Economy

Cultural Factors

India has been one of the most complex of countries. It has a continuity of cultural heritage that extends back to millenia. It has perhaps the largest prehistoric tribes; Dravidians, Aryands, Negroids and mongoloids; a land that has gone through a stage of intense intermingling of ethnic groups unparalleled in history and a home to four religions, Hinduism, Buddhism, Jainism and Sikhism. Then came Christianity 2000 years back (in 53AD) and later Islam introduced by the invasion of Mughal emperors. It has witnessed the growth of systems of social organisations through the centuries, like caste, joint family and autonomous village communities. And has gone through diverse types of feudal order such as monarchs, kings, zamindars, etc. It has borne the stamp of the dominant ruling class. Myths, symbols, legends, philosophies and religious beliefs furthered only their interests. The seven main domains of culture are language, morality, esthetic expression, myth, religion, philosophy and science.

Indian culture is heavily influenced by Religion. Many aspects of Indian culture, such as the caste system, have their origins in religion. As a major religion Hinduism has a significant influence on Indian Politics and culture. Indian culture is one of the oldest cultures in the world, and it has been influenced by a variety of religions. While Indian culture is heavily influenced by religion, it is also secular, with many people not practising any religion. Indian culture is also very diverse, with different regions of the country having their own unique cultures. Culture is the bloodstream of the social life of the people. Therefore if we must create a better future we must first know our past and its relation to the present.

Remember how the cultural revolution in China changed its lifestyle, policies and outlook.

Socialism

After the first world war, socialist ideologies were being considered by the Indian Intelligentsia. Socialism is considered midway between capitalism and communism. The rise of the Labour party in Britain and the Russian Revolution in 1917 and other communist movements that fought for the rights of the working class, sought to eradicate the capitalist philosophy. But these ideals could not make the desired impact on the rigidly religious minded and illiterate masses of India. Communism was rejected because it was equal to godliness. Though every Politician professes to be a Gandhian, they were motivated by selfishness, hunger for power, greed for wealth and not truly interested in the emancipation of the poor. Through the 1955 Avadi Resolution of the Indian National Congress, a socialistic pattern of development was presented as the goal of the party. Nehru, first leader of independent India, was an avowed socialist. A year later, the Indian parliament adopted 'socialistic pattern of development' as official policy, a policy that came to include land reforms and regulations of industries. Thus Socialism was acknowledged as the cherished goal of the Indian political system in its constitution. After independence and until the early 1990s, socialism shaped some economic and social policies of the Indian government. Later, India moved towards a 'market based economy' and privatisation of some poorly performing state companies. Foreign direct investment also began with caution.

Economy

A capitalist system automatically creates Black money. This happens especially in the Film industry where actors are paid in crores, business dealings transactions and bribing the politicians or government officials to get contracts or other favours. The main cause of massive poverty was the unjust socio-economic policies whereby the resources available to the society were used only to satisfy the never ending needs of a few elite, while the basic needs of the poor millions go unattended. Corruption, cronyism, nepotism, investment and divestment based on patronage have kept India down.

Soon after independence, the government chose to protect the Indian goods ('Closed economy') and did not permit multinational manufacturers. Even the then Singapore PM Lee advised India to open up the market. But, China with a communist regime, permitted multinational manufacturing units with all facilities (as low labour cost, supply chains, transport, easy permits, low taxes, etc.) and exported the products to all countries, thereby earning much foreign exchange ('open economy'). It became known as the 'World Factory'. You pick-up any item (dress, toys, electronic goods, home equipment, etc.) in the USA, Canada, Europe and check the label to be 'Made in China'. While India lags behind China and Southeast Asian countries in terms of manufacturing competitiveness, red tape, corruption, stiff regulatory permits,high land rates, electricity tariffs, and a 33 percent corporate tax rate have hindered India's competitiveness. Thus, China became an Economic super power. So by not allowing the foreign brands to 'Make in India', we lost that chance to be a great Economy, missed out on giving employment to so many engineers, technical workers and labourers and raise the status of common man. Recently India (under PM Modi's rule) has raised slogans like 'Make in India' or 'Clean India' to attract foreign companies. But they remain as mere slogans.

CHAPTER V

India–the Present Status

Literacy

According to the latest data (As compared to the last census in 2011), the literacy rate in India has increased by 5% in 2023 to 77.7%. The present literacy rate is about 76% below China which has 99%. According to a UNESCO report, India hopes universal literacy in the year 2060. Kerala has the highest literacy rate in India, with an impressive 96.2%. This research article examines the state-wise literacy rates in India, with a focus on male and female literacy, as well as the disparities between them. The data was sourced from a survey conducted by the National Statistical Office (NSO), with a special emphasis on Union Territories and Northeastern states based on the 2011 Census. Kerala boasts the highest literacy rate at 96.2%, while Andhra Pradesh reports the lowest at 66.4%. Notably, the national male-female literacy gap stands at 12.9%. Kerala also demonstrates the smallest gender gap at 2.2%, while Rajasthan exhibits the highest at 23.3%. Through descriptive and exploratory analysis, this article provides a comprehensive overview of literacy rates across various Indian states and Union Territories, highlighting the significant disparities that exist. (Literacy rate in India in 2023 by Khritish Swargiary. ResearchGate 2023).

Healthcare

According to Health and health care systems, ranking of countries worldwide in 2021, by health index score India was ranked 111 out of 167 countries. India's public expenditure on healthcare is only 2.1% of GDP in 2021-22 while Japan, Canada and France spend about 10% of their GDP on public healthcare. One of the major weaknesses of the Indian healthcare system is inadequate infrastructure. The country's healthcare infrastructure, particularly in rural areas, is inadequate to meet the growing healthcare needs of the population. According to the National Health Profile, India has only 0.9 beds per 1000 population and out of which only 30% are in rural areas.

Inadequate access to basic healthcare services such as shortage of medical professionals, a lack of quality assurance, insufficient health spending, and, most significantly, insufficient research funding. In India, there is a shortage of doctors, nurses, and other healthcare professionals. According to a study presented in Parliament by a minister, India is short 600,000 doctors. Factors affecting health in India: Natural factors such as air, water, soil pollution, radiation and noise, Social factors such as income, education, political and economic system in the society, social and cultural system and lack of preventative health care services.

Poverty

Poverty is the state of not having enough material possessions or income for a person's basic needs. Poverty may include social, economic, and political elements. Absolute poverty is the complete lack of the means necessary to meet basic personal needs, such as food, clothing, and shelter. As the fourth largest Economic power, it is a paradox that about 15% are in the state of mult-dimensional poverty. The clock has taken $2.15 a day income to present the finding. Accordingly, nearly 3.44 crore people are living in extreme population in 2024 against 4.69 crore in 2022. Poverty is the state of not having enough material possessions or income for a person's basic needs. Poverty may include social, economic, and political elements. Absolute poverty is the complete lack of the means necessary to meet basic personal needs, such as food, clothing, and shelter.

Using the $3.20 per day poverty line, the percentage of the population living in poverty in India was 60% in 2011. This means that 763 million people in India were very poor. According to Niti Aayog, approximately 14.96% of India's population is considered to be in a state of multidimensional poverty. The National Multidimensional Poverty Index (MPI) assesses simultaneous deprivations in health, education, and standard of living, with each dimension carrying equal weight. According to the World Food program, around 21.25% of India's population live on less than US$1.90 a day. The WFP also says that India is home to a quarter of the world's undernourished people. States like Bihar, Jharkhand and Meghalaya had the highest share of the multidimensionally poor population in 2019-2021, the latest data that has been shared.

Maharashtra: India's wealthiest state GDP for the year 2023-24 is Rs 38.79 Lakh crore, according to Forbes.

Tamil Nadu: Holds the second position in the list with its GDP for the year 2023-24 valuing at Rs 28.03 Lakh crore.

Bihar is one of the lowest GDP states in India with a contribution of only Rs 8.6 lakh crore, about 3.1% to India's overall GDP. The state has struggled with poverty, unemployment, and underdeveloped infrastructure, which has hindered its economic growth

Maharashtra tops the overall ranking of all states, with a favourable score in social, financial inclusion and fiscal categories. Gujarat ranks second and fares well in economic and fiscal categories, while Tamil Nadu ranks third with an edge in social and governance categories.

After fifty years of development, mass poverty still persists in India. This analysis attempts to bring out how various sectors of the economy impinge on the development process. The key features to the elimination of poverty in India are transferring labour from agriculture to industry and growth in agricultural productivity. Industrial progress cannot benefit the poor in the absence of progress in the agricultural sector. By exporting industrial goods, the labour force employed in agriculture can be reduced and the poor in India would be made better off. Finally, 'it is argued that

India's industrial policy from Independence until very recently was designed to stifle entrepreneurship and undermine technical advancement' (Mukesh Eashwaran 1997).

Rich-Poor divide

In India, 'Rich - Poor divide' is very extreme. While millionaires or billionaires live very luxurious life in large mansions with a fleet of cars, paying the same rate of income tax as ordinary people, while the poor live in dilapidated temporary sheds without basic necessities such as electricity, water supply, drainage, etc. Inequality has been rising in India and the top 1% billionaires hold 40% of the wealth. The middle class and government servants contribute most of the income tax. Income inequality is there. The number of Indians with net wealth exceeding $1 billion rose from one in 1991 to 162 in 2022. Asia's two richest men, Reliance Industries' Mukesh Ambani and Adani Group's Gautam Adani are Indian. The 10,000 wealthiest individuals of the 92 million Indian adults own an average of Rs.22.6 billion in wealth—16,763 times the country's average—while the top 1 percent possess an average of Rs.54 million in wealth, its highest in six decades. India's main opposition party, the Congress has raised the issue of Modi's government's closeness to billionaires and their contributions for his party BJP in return for favours.

Economic condition

India is performing well economically, with strong growth projections for the coming years. Key drivers include robust domestic demand, a growing middle class and a recovering services sector. India is also a major and growing exporter of goods and services and a major recipient of foreign direct investment. The IMF's numbers for 2024 put India's GDP at $3.94 trillion (in nominal dollars), only fractionally smaller than Japan's at $4.11 trillion. India is in the 139th position in the League of Nations in terms of per capita income.

Taking all five years together (2019-2024), average annual growth has been only 4.5%. That is slower than in any previous quinquennium of the last three decades. Over the Modi decade (2014–24), growth has been slower than in the Manmohan Singh decade (2004-2014) that went before; though such comparisons are somewhat unfair.

Even providing for such factors, there are plenty of worrying trends to consider. The economy has turned more inward-looking, judging by the sharp reduction in the ratio between external trade and GDP. The exports of goods and services, in relation to the size of the economy, have shrunk to about 21% from 30%. This is rarely a positive development–almost all rapidly-growing economies have been outward-looking. On top of that, there is the consumption slowdown. Public debt is high too, at 82% of GDP (compared with a desirable 60%, as recommended by a committee), and will of necessity constrain future government borrowing. To this writer, the odds on that still look quite long.

Yet, many constraints are already obvious: the poor educational attainments and health metrics of the bulk of the population, the failure at a national level to move surplus workers on farms to higher-productivity jobs in the manufacturing and service sectors, and the vulnerability that comes with extreme external dependence for energy. Key developmental and structural transitions are therefore yet to be achieved. Educated unemployment is still at extraordinarily high levels. Wage levels too have shown little or no improvement. Income inequality has to be removed. The second issue is inflation. This suggests widespread economic distress, or at the least frustrated hopes.

India is ranked only 63rd out of 190 countries in the World Bank's 2020 ease of doing business index. In terms of dealing with construction permits and enforcing contracts, it is ranked among the 10 worst in the world. India has a parallel underground economy, with a 2006 report alleging that India topped the worldwide list for black money with almost $1,456 billion stashed in Swiss banks.

The World Inequality Lab has documented a significant rise in economic disparities in India. Nearly 90 per cent of the country's billionaire wealth has been found concentrated in the hands of the upper castes who hold nearly 55 per cent of the national wealth, according to the All-India Debt and Investment Survey (AIDIS) for 2018-19. This stark contrast in wealth ownership underscores the deep-seated economic inequalities rooted in India's caste system. Upper castes constitute 15-20% of India's population but are over represented in every walk of Indian society.

Economic Offenders

As many as 38 economic offenders who defaulted on repaying hefty borrowed amounts to banks fled the country in a span of five years, starting January 1, 2015 to Dec 31, 2019. Industrialist Vijay Mallya secretly left the country to settle in the UK, he took an estimated Rs 9,091 crore in loans from public sector banks. Mehul Choksi, a runaway businessman residing in Antigua and Barbuda, is being sought by Indian authorities for accusations of criminal conspiracies, breach of trust, and money laundering. He previously owned Gitanjali Group, a retail jewellery corporation with 4,000 branches throughout India. Choksi is suspected to have allegedly collaborated with two Punjab National Bank (PNB) employees in a $1.8 billion scam. Fashion designer and diamond jeweller Nirav Modi is a fugitive businessman wanted by Indian authorities for his alleged involvement in a multi-crore Punjab National Bank (PNB) fraud case. He is accused of defrauding the bank of over $2 billion in collusion with some of its employees. He too escaped from India in January 2018. How were they allowed to flee the country? Owner of Gujarat-based Sterling Biotech, Nitin J. Sandesara has defaulted on the ?5,000 crore loaned to Andhra Bank. The swindle ended up costing Rs 81,000 crore.

Corruption

India is at 93rd position among 180 countries, in the Corruption Perception Index for the year 2023, with a score of 39, dropping from 85th position in 2022. The list of scams and scandals in the country is endless. Many of the biggest scandals since 2010 have involved high level government officials, including Cabinet Ministers and Chief Ministers, such as the 2010 Commonwealth Games scam (?70,000 crore (US$8.8 billion)), the Adarsh Housing Society scam, the Coal Mining Scam (?1.86 lakh crore (US$23 billion)), the Mining Scandal, 2010 Commonwealth games scam (70,000 crore/US$ 8.4 billion), Electoral bond scam, Cash-for-vote scams. The Bofors payoff scandal of 1986 involved a total amount of Rs 1750 crore in purchase of guns from a Swedish firm for the Army. The Cement scandal of 1982, the Sugar Scandal of 1994, the Urea Scam, Hawala Scandal of 1991, the Coffin-gate fodder scam in Bihar or the Stamp scandal which shocked not only the political arena but the entire society. For three years in a row, Rajasthan and Maharashtra remain the states with the most corruption cases in the country, as per the 2022 annual report of the National Crime Records Bureau (NCRB). At least one in every two people in India have paid a bribe in the past year. My personal experience is Corruption is high in North and least in Kerala where there is high literacy rate of 94%.

The causes of corruption in India include excessive regulations, complicated tax and licensing systems, numerous government departments with opaque bureaucracy and discretionary powers, monopoly of government controlled institutions on certain goods and services delivery, low paid government employees, and the lack of transparent laws and processes

Anang Pal Malik (2016) in his book '**Corruption in India**' gives a hard hitting account on the growing malpractice of bribery, He methodically proves that - 1. In India, at least 90% of those who have opportunities to be corrupt are corrupt and, the corrupt dislike being termed as such in public. 2. The families of corrupt do not consider this menace of corruption a crime in the least. The book correlates corruption with socialism, which keeps the salaries of government servants low but at the same time vests them with enormous power to financially thrive on the misfortunes of the common man. The book is an eye opener and a precise account on how despite having laws, nothing can be achieved till the society takes up a stand against it. Author gets to the root of corruption in India, exposing the magnitude of corruption and how and why it crippled India for decades and centuries.

Presently, India figures as the **seventh most corrupt country** in the world according to Transparency International', a non-government German Organization. Acceptance of gifts and rewards for work done in an official capacity, or obtaining objects or advantages, iIllegally, or fraudulent use of public property, acquiring financial resources more than one's income, abuse of public office, avoiding one's duty or avoiding payment of taxes are a few kinds of corruption prevalent in our society today. It is also at a high rate in departments like Communication, Defence, Public Works, Police, Excise and Revenue. Corruption in these departments is rampant at all levels from the highest to the lowest. It is well established that politicians are extremely corrupt in developing countries. In fact, people are surprised to find an honest politician. These corrupt politicians go scot-free and unpunished because of their influence and power. Even some judges are corrupt. Corruption is there in levels, top to bottom in each department. Without bribing nothing can be done. Public works, Revenue, Land or house approvals and registration, new connections for water supply, electricity, etc are the most corrupt. The anti-corruption departments in India exist as defunct outfits. Though laws exist, enforcement is not there or poor. For traffic violations, mostly police take bribes.

Corruption in the Indian education system has been eroding the quality of education and has been creating long-term negative consequences for the society. Educational corruption in India is considered one of the major contributors to domestic black money.

In North India, any degree can be bought. In 2021, a private university in Bihar, was accused of selling tens of thousands of degrees for money over a decade. In the name of donations, money is demanded for even nursery and professional colleges (engineering or medicine) in lakhs.

CHAPTER VI

The Great Indian Brain Drain

Emigration

In India, brain drain has become a significant concern due to the steady departure of talented individuals seeking better opportunities abroad. In 2020, there were 2 crore Indians living overseas. Notably, between 2016 and 2020, 6 lakh Indians renounced their citizenship, as India does not allow dual citizenship and since 2011, over 1.6 million people have relinquished their Indian citizenship leading to loss of billions in tax revenue for India.. According to an Expat Insider 2021 survey, 59% of Indians moved abroad for their careers, more than 10% higher than the global average of 47%. This in itself sounds very arbitrary but when you start to drill down multiple causative factors come into play. During the great Indian migration wave, spanning the past 150 years, more than 100 million people have migrated for work, which makes a fifth of the total workforce in India. What are the main reasons for brain drain in India?

Lack Of Opportunity in Higher Education

One of the reasons for Indian students moving abroad is the inferior standard of education, high cost of higher education and the tough competition to get into premiere Indian universities. I wished to pursue my higher studies abroad since I secured first class and first rank in Madras University in my Master's degree. But due to financial constraint and lack of opportunity, I was not able to achieve my wish.

Employment opportunities, Higher pay with quality life

The job market in India is highly competitive. Many Indians have friends or family living overseas and they share stories with their families back in India of how their lives have changed for the better. The infrastructure, social welfare, most advanced healthcare, equitable pay, quality of life, clean environment, greenery, uncorrupted society and so on. These stories have surely planted seeds in the minds of many young Indians, who have made migrating overseas their life's biggest dream. Though there may be cases of racial discrimination yet, several Indians continue to want to work overseas.

Many prominent Indians like Nadella of Microsoft, Sundar Pitchai of Google, Rishi Sunak-PM of UK, and many others have achieved the top posts. There, their talents of the workforce are recognised, while in India they are suppressed by the caste, race issue and due the hierarchical system. It is evidenced, as Professor Ramesh Thakur rightly said, by the fact that it is "easier for a person of Indian origin to reach high public office in Canada, Ireland, the United Kingdom and the U.S" than in India. The current work environment has become stressful with long working hours, lack of job security, low wages, and growing competition. Indian culture is mentally toxic and exhausting. Talking of ranking index of powerful passports of the world: India passport ranking as per the Henley Passport Index 2024, is ranked at the 81st position, with access to 61 countries. India's passport ranking in the global passport rankings 2024 reflects our global standing and the citizens' ease of access regarding international travel.

CHAPTER VII

Happiness-why life is pitiable?

Unhappiness

India is ranked 126th out of 143 nations in the World Happiness Report (WHR) recently released on March 20, 2024, the UN's International Day of Happiness. "Despite our country's economic progress, India is constantly going downwards in the happiness index. This indicates a lack of holistic approach towards development," said a former President in 2018. The picture about India's happiness quotient presented by this report is quite disappointing. In broad terms, the rankings are loosely correlated with countries' prosperity, but other factors such as life expectancy, social bonds, personal freedom, and corruption appear to influence individuals' assessments too. The young in India are the "happiest" lot while those in the "lower middle" rung are the least happy. India is also in the 139th position in the league of Nations in terms of per capita income.

Cleanliness

A new report on the fitness level of Indians has found that 45% of the country's population hovered dangerously close to being classified as "unhealthy" in 2023. Why? It's only because of uncleanness and pollution. Air quality is also poor, with dust, smoke (exhaust for poorly maintained automobiles) and other pollutants. A Swiss study showed 39 of the world's most polluted cities are in India. The cleanest countries in the world are known for their exemplary environmental performance, including outstanding air and water quality, effective waste management systems, and robust policies on pollution control and sustainable practices. These nations often achieve high scores in global environmental indices and are committed to renewable energy and conservation efforts, maintaining pristine natural landscapes and healthy living conditions for their citizens. The top five countries are Denmark, United Kingdom, Finland, Malta and Sweden. India ranked last at 180th position with a score of only 18.9. Poor unhygienic living standards, low per capita income, high taxes, air-water-soil pollution, income inequality, unemployment, stressful education system, corruption, poverty, rigid traditions, superstitions, exploitation, social prejudice, caste system, discrimination on basis of caste, language and religion, inadequate infrastructure, poor health care, high population density, lack of social support, rich-poor divide, child abuse, child labour and bonded labour, etc.

M.Kiran on Quora tells "Most of the streets are filthy; People lack civic sense. They don't consider their own garbage as their own responsibility. This basically stems from the dysfunctional education system. Widespread corruption in both public and private domains of life: Institutionalised corruption in government and nepotism and exploitation and pathetic work culture in the private sector. Retrogressive society - Rigid social systems like caste system which alienates fellow countrymen based on imaginary ideals like caste supremacy. Influence of Religion, Caste, Race in every damn thing; High rate of unemployment and underemployment; Outdated and utterly dysfunctional old Education System which needs a major revamp; Hate Politics and Crooked Politicians dividing people using Caste and Religion."

Punctuality, Discipline and Efficiency

E.M.Forster's famous novel '**A Passage to India**' (1924) stated that India is where "adventures do occur, but not punctually." Our lack of punctuality is so infamous that the acronym IST, which stands for Indian Standard Time, is often jokingly expanded as Indian

Stretchable Time! It is common for people to arrive at events 30 minutes to an hour after the designated time, whether it is a meeting or banks or government office or a function or Prayer service in church/temple or any event.

Indians are always blamed for not being punctual, this also affects their reputation on the clients of other countries. Also over the years it has been observed that Indians always have a casual attitude towards punctuality. Trains always run late, never in time. There is a joke that one day a train was very punctual and a passenger was surprised telling another, 'Today it is surprising that the train is very punctual'. In reply, the other person said that it was yesterday's train, running 24 hours late! The website 'Exactly What Is Time?' states: 'It is not unusual for trains in India to be several hours, or even a full day, late, without creating undue stress and turmoil', adding that 'such cultures, with thousands of years of history behind them, have such a long point of view that time at the scale of minutes, or even hours, becomes insignificant and inconsequential'.

Punctuality and efficiency issues in India have always been a major concern, but still the majority of the population continues to follow their habit of not being punctual. For example in every field we have punctuality issues like for example be it the Indian railways, air service, bus services or the other development projects as such. In the public sectors or the Indian government departments, your work will never be done in time, it will keep delaying and a very simple work might also take years to get completed. If bribed, it will be done. The employees always come late or even never come and most of the time chat and do little work. Punctuality in India has been the biggest concern in every field. We do not like to be ruled by the clock. Indians definitely have good regards for the people who are punctual in their work, but they never try to adapt this habit themselves, except a few. It's high time, people in India should value time. Time management is the key to success. Indian's should now become active and leave their habit of not being punctual, which has been continuing for several years. Missing deadlines, appointments and the habit of laziness will not take you even close to success. You should value your time, each and every second is precious.

We also lack discipline, whether on road, walking or driving, in public places, in school/college campuses, in parking vehicles, in shopping malls, in parks, tourist spots, religious places, and so on. Parking on both sides of a narrow road leads to traffic congestion. There is no traffic sense and no road/speed/signal rules are followed. Jumping red signals is common in the absence of policing. No lane discipline even on highways. Though vehicles should overtake only on the right side, they overtake any side they like. On curves and turns, they don't keep left. Two wheelers are the worst offenders, driving fast wherever they like. Pedestrians too cross roads wherever they like. Excessive unwarranted use of loud noisy horns irritates one. They even honk on signals turning green or in slow moving traffic conditions. Overspeeding goes unchecked. Kids, minors as young as 10 years old and teenagers without driving licenses are often seen driving 2 wheelers on interior streets or roads. Three wheeler autos carry an overload of kids to school or the whole family with two kids ride on 2-wheelers.

Coughing, sneezing are done openly in public places or in buses or trains. without using a handkerchief. They also spit or blow noses or spit the chewing tobacco-betel paste that is reddish coloured anywhere they want, on road sides, public places, parks, subways, rarely on rail platforms too. People also have the habit of spitting while driving a two wheeler, causing inconvenience on the person coming behind; he is sprayed with that saliva. Garbage, litter, organic waste are dumped on street sides, open fallows and anywhere they like. They urinate wherever they want, on roadsides, wastelands, even on compound walls of bus stations, where one has to use 'Pay and Use' washrooms or free dirty washrooms which may be dirty and stinking.

High population density in urban areas coupled with shortage of public service transports (buses, metros. trains) lead to overcrowded or footboard or overboard travel. Hence, while boarding buses, metros or inter-city trains, no order or discipline. There is pushing and pulling to enter first to occupy seats. Queue system is not followed anywhere. Recently in Chennai train station (June 2024), even passengers with reserved tickets were unable to board as the unauthorised people (without reservation or even without proper tickets barged into reserved coaches first. This situation is very common in the North. The Railway Minister expressed concern over the surge in complaints of overcrowding in reserved coaches and against unauthorised passengers. In buses and metros, people occupy seats marked for 'ladies' and never offer seats for standing mothers with babies or elderly.

Dishonesty and Cheating

Although corruption, hacking, and cybercrime are worldwide phenomena, more people are cheated in India, especially due to cybercrimes. Even the government cheats people. Though the cost recovered long ago, toll plazas on highways in Tamil Nadu still continue to collect toll, despite objections from the state government and all major political parties. This is nothing but cheating and daylight robbery by the BJP ruled Central government. Trichy-Madurai section of National Highway 38 was built at a cost of Rs 419 crore. However, since the toll collection started in 2010, the two toll booths have together collected Rs 1,202 crore as of November 2023. Similar is the case of Chennai Bypass, which was built at an expenditure of Rs 446 crore, the toll plazas have already collected Rs 1,341 crore as of March 2024.

Most of the business owners or shopkeepers are dishonest. They never give proper bills or give false or fake or handwritten slips bills. This to escape paying commercial or goods-service taxes. They get cheated through fake emails from individuals or Fedex or DHL promising gifts or shares in their wealth, asking for bank details. (I have too received such emails or calls and was nearly cheated). Mobiles with whatsapp and other banking apps made it easy for these cyber-criminals to send SMS, call or hack mobiles.

Many people have lost lakhs of rupees. Another complaint is 'cheating' the customers in shopping or in hiring three-wheeler taxis (autos) or private cabs. Foreign tourists are worst affected. But in my experience, three wheeler taxi drivers never cheat in Kerala. Customers depositing recurring amounts in private chit funds that make false benefits are also suddenly cheated. One fine day, the chit funds or persons collecting money disappear. This is very common in India only. There are many fake doctors or 'quack doctors' exploiting the poor and illiterate. Supporting WHO's report, the Indian Medical Association (IMA) claims that India has about 1 million quacks performing medicine among which 600,000 offer allopathic treatments.

Food adulteration

This is also very common in India. Food adulteration refers to the alteration of food quality that takes place deliberately. It includes the addition of ingredients to modify different properties of food products for economic advantage and profit maximisation. Adulterated food products are responsible for mild to severe health impacts as well as financial damage. Diarrhoea, nausea, allergic reaction, diabetes, cardiovascular disease, etc., are frequently observed illnesses upon consumption of adulterated food. Some adulterants have shown carcinogenic, clastogenic, and genotoxic properties. Adulterated stuff is neatly packed with reliable brand names. It is difficult to find the difference between original and fake spurious products. For example, black pepper is adulterated with dry papaya seeds; Tea powder with saw dust; Coffee powder with roasted/powdered tamarind seeds, barley or chicory; Rice or pulses with small stones. Milk with water. Turmeric powder is adulterated with chalk powder or Starch is added to the volume of the turmeric powder. Adulteration with preservatives, colourants, and artificial sweeteners are also common food adulteration techniques. Artificial ripening of fruits especially banana, mangoes, etc. the carcinogenic chemicals as Calcium carbide or ethylene. Food adulteration rate in India has almost doubled over the last 5 years. The huge increase in the detection of food adulteration cases across India — from 15 per cent in 2012-2013 to 28 per cent in 2018-2019, as per the Food Safety and Standards Authority of India (FSSAI) — should be a sign of worry and serious concern. The latest data on food items show that nearly 50% of the food consumed every day is adulterated.

Are Indian streets safe?

What rank is India in safety? India is ranked 126th on the list. The GPI considers 23 indicators including societal safety and security. On October 23, 2023, Parag Desai, the executive director of one of India's largest tea companies fell and fatally hit his head as he was trying to flee from a pack of street dogs in the city of Ahmedabad. The problem of street dogs has long been a matter of debate between animal lovers and victims. This of course comes after multiple reports of people, many of them children, being attacked and killed by dogs. While some of this is media hysteria, the data is clear that dogs are actually a major problem in India's cities. I was once attacked from the back and bitten in the lower leg by a dog while walking on a street and sometimes stray dogs also bark at me. Around 36% of all rabies deaths in the world are from India. In effect, an Indian is, on average, twice as likely to die from rabies compared to a person from any other country. In the case of the other animal that dominates Indian streets, the cow, religious and political sentiments around the animal override any dangers they pose to commuters. This is in spite of the fact that stray cattle are now a major issue in states in North and Western India. In Haryana for example, nearly a thousand people have been killed in accidents involving stray cattle in the past five years.

On almost any parameter, an Indian city offers a terrible quality of life. Indian cities, for example, have the worst traffic indiscipline and congestion, with pedestrians, cycles, two wheelers, three wheeler taxis, cars, trucks, buses criss-crossing on the roads. There is no lane discipline or speed limits.India's urban population is an incredible 675 million – twice that of the entire population of the United States. So just in terms of human welfare, improving its cities should be an important goal.

India can boast of having the world's highest number of road accidents and deaths. India universally has the highest number of road fatalities each year, being 2,50,000 deaths a year. As per the 2022 Annual report of the Ministry of Road transport and Highways, a total of 4,61,312 road accidents have been reported in India in 2022, which claimed 1,68,491 lives and caused injuries to 4,43,366 persons. This marks an increase of 11.9% in accidents, 9.4% in fatalities, and 15.3% in injuries compared to the previous year. The report underscores the urgency of adopting a comprehensive approach to address the contributing factors to these accidents, including speeding, reckless driving, drunken driving, and non-compliance with traffic regulations.

Are women and children safe?

Women and kids are not fully secure on Indian streets, especially at night. Children are kidnapped on roads and young women are also kidnapped and raped, and also killed at times. Even newborn babies in hospitals are stolen and sold. Women walking on lonely streets with a hand-bag, mobile in hand, and gold chains are snatched by bikers. Even old women living alone are not safe. The 2012 Delhi 5 member gang rape and murder, commonly known as the Nirbhaya case, involved a rape and fatal assault on a 22 year old student who travelled at night in a city bus with her male mate and 5 other passengers who raped her. In Kerala, 16-year-old girl who was raped by a number of different men for 40 days in 1996. Between 1996 and 2006, a cop turned serial rapist, Umesh did terrible things to women, such as raping, robbing and murdering some 20 women in Karnataka, Maharashtra and Gujarat. Uttar Pradesh leads in crimes against women in absolute numbers, while Kolkata remains the safest metropolis for three consecutive years. Pseudoscientific practices and Godmen misleading and exploiting people (especially women) and their unholy nexus with politicians is deplorable.

The National Crime Records Bureau's (NCRB) annual report reveals a harrowing surge in crimes against women in India. With a staggering 4,45,256 cases registered in 2022 alone, equivalent to nearly 51 FIRs every hour. The rate of crimes against women per lakh population stood at 66.4. A total of 28,522 FIRs of murder were registered in 2022—an average of 78 killings every day or more than three every hour. The rate of murder per lakh population across the country stood at 2.1.

Child labour

In India, millions of children are forced into child labour due to poverty, high illiteracy rates due to lack of education, unemployment, overpopulation, etc. The term 'child labour' is best defined as work that deprives children of their childhood, their potential and their dignity, and that is harmful to physical and mental development. Interferes with their schooling by depriving them of the opportunity to attend school; obliging them to leave school prematurely; or requiring them to attempt to combine school attendance with excessively long and heavy work. In 2014, the U.S. Department of Labor issued a List of Goods Produced by Child Labor or Forced Labor and India figured among 74 countries where a significant incidence of critical working conditions has been observed. Unlike any other country, 23 goods were attributed to India, the majority of which are produced by child labour in the manufacturing sector.

It is a complex problem that is rooted in poverty. Since the 1990s, the government has implemented a variety of laws and programs to eliminate child labour. These have included setting up schools, launching free school lunch programs, creating special investigation cells, etc. Recent studies on child labour in India have found some pockets of industries in which children are employed, but overall, relatively few Indian children are employed. Child labour below the age of 10 is now rare. In the 10–14 age group, theThe presence of a large number of child labourers is regarded as a serious issue in terms of economic welfare. Children who work fail to get necessary education. They do not get the opportunity to develop physically, intellectually, emotionally and psychologically. In terms of the physical condition of children, children are not ready for long monotonous work because they become exhausted more quickly than adults. This reduces their physical conditions and makes the children more vulnerable to disease.

Children in hazardous working conditions, such as in the fireworks manufacture sector, are even in worse condition. Child labour is significant in Tamil Nadu's fireworks, matches or incense sticks industries. Children who work, instead of going to school, will remain illiterate which limits their ability to contribute to their own well-being as well as to the community they live in. Child labour has long term adverse effects for India. latest surveys find only 2% of children working for wage, while another 9% work within their home or rural farms assisting their parents in times of high work demand such as sowing and harvesting of crops. As reported by Save the Children, children between the ages of 14 and 17 years engage in hazardous work and account for 62.8% of India's child labour workforce in which more boys than girls (38.7 million vs. 8.8 million) are forced into doing more hazardous work

Still worse problem is Bonded child labour is a system of forced, or partly forced, labour under which the child, or child's parent enter into an agreement, oral or written, with a creditor. The child performs work as in-kind repayment of credit.

CHAPTER VIII

Indian Politics and Politicians

The functioning of the political system is crucial for the smooth development of any country. In its annual report on global political rights and liberties, US-based non-profit Freedom House downgraded India from a free democracy to a "partially free democracy". Then Sweden-based V-Dem Institute was harsher in its latest report on democracy, stating India had become an "**electoral autocracy**". And last month, India, described as a "**flawed or defective democracy**", slipped two places to 53rd position in the latest Democracy Index published by The Economist Intelligence Unit. From 2006 to 2024 the situation of Indian democracy worsened still.

The rankings blame Mr Modi and his Hindu nationalist Bhartiya JP government for the backsliding of democracy. Under Mr Modi's watch, they say, there has been increased pressure on human rights groups, intimidation of journalists and activists, and a spate of attacks, especially against Christians and Muslims. Criticism against his policies are not tolerated. No press meet has been conducted during the last 10 years of his term as PM. This, they add, has led to a deterioration of political and civil liberties in the country.

Political parties in India are generally of two major categories, these are National Parties and Regional parties. Although a strict anti-defection law had been passed in 1984, there has been a continued tendency amongst politicians to float their own parties rather than join a broad based party such as the Congress or the BJP. Between the 1984 and 1989 elections, the number of parties contesting elections increased from 33 to 113. In the decades since, this fragmentation has continued. The elected political leaders are not the people's representatives in general-they are stooges of party politics. Many of them have no principle and change parties like a man changing his shirt. To topple elected governments with little majority, leaders are heavily bribed to change party (defection).

Freedom of Press

A free and independent press serves as a vital check on the actions of governments and administrative bodies, for a healthy democracy. Since the last few years, criticism of the government policies or its leaders have not been tolerated. Press freedom has eroded rapidly in recent years, with India ranked as low as 161 out of 180 nations last year, the lowest ever for the country. In the span of 30 years from 1992 to 2022, about 25 journalists have been imprisoned for various reasons like criticism, reporting on rapes, caste violence, religious freedom, government persecution of journalists. Physical Threats and Violence against Journalists are there. Recent case of journalist S.Kappan's arrest in 2020 is an example. Particularly when they report on sensitive issues like corruption or communal tensions, tragically, some journalists have paid the ultimate price, facing attacks or even losing their lives while fulfilling their professional duties.

Political violence

The culture of political violence in India is not new. It is the violence which is perpetrated by people, by political parties or governments in order to achieve political goals. Political violence encompasses those violent acts which result from attempts either to change or resist change to a country's political system or aspects of it. It is a broad category which includes violent demonstrations, riots of a political nature, insurrections, and assassinations. Politicians often capitalise on the emotions and beliefs of common people that can be regional, ethnic, and religious. They become an integral part of the political process. These values and beliefs become extremely intense and often lead to violence in the struggle for political supremacy. According to the latest NCRB report of 2021, West Bengal has recorded the highest number of political murders in the country, and the rates are also notable in states like Kerala, Jharkhand, and West Bengal. The highest numbers of overall murders are in Uttar Pradesh and Bihar. The number of victims of political violence in our country is much higher than the number of deaths due to terror attacks.

The assassination of a particular leader of a politically motivated community during the election period began with the 1985 General Elections in Bihar when 63 people, including four candidates, were killed and 200 people were seriously injured.The same was repeated in the next general elections. Between 1990 and 2004, as reported, almost 644 people lost their lives in various elections in Bihar.

Another gruesome case took place in Dharmapuri when a political party protesters set fire to the Tamil Nadu Agricultural University bus. Three students were burned to death, and 16 others were injured. For misuse of office of chief minister of Tamil nadu state and for her lavish marriage of her foster son in 1996 and her acquisition of properties worth more than ?66.65 crore (equivalent to ?364 crore or US$44 million in 2023), as well as jewellery, cash deposits, investments and a fleet of luxury cars, Miss Jayalalitha was fined Rs 100 crores and four year imprisonment in 2014. This was the first case where a ruling chief minister had to step down on account of a court sentence. Ultimately on appeal to the high court, in 2015, her conviction was overturned, she was acquitted of all charges, and she then died before the Supreme Court of India reviewed the case in 2017 and convicted her associates. Announcement of the judgement and sentence was delayed by six hours, leading to chaos outside the court. Soon after, sporadic incidents of violence as arson,looting, attack on public property, and burning public buses were reported across the state initiated by her party workers.

Does the Political system of India cheat the common people?

D K Srivastava, a senior lawyer of Mumbai High Court, posted the below message on social media for wide publicity:-
Does the system of India cheat the common people?

1- If a political leader wants, he can contest elections from two seats simultaneously! But....

You cannot vote at two places.

2- If you are in jail, you cannot vote.. But a political leader can contest elections while being in jail.

3- If you have ever gone to jail, now you will not get any government job for the rest of your life,But...No matter how many times a leader has gone to jail in a case of murder or rape, he can still become the Prime Minister or President,

4- To get a simple job in a bank, You must be a graduate..But, Even if a leader is illiterate, he can become the Finance Minister of India.

5-To get a job of a simple soldier in the army, you have to show that you can run 10 kilometres with a degree, but....even if a leader is illiterate and crippled, he can still become the head of Army, Navy and Air Force, i.e. Defense Minister.

6- A leader whose entire family has never gone to school, can become the Education Minister of the country.

7- A leader who has thousands of cases pending against him, can become the Chief of Police Department, i.e. Home Minister.

If you feel that this system should be changed, there should be only one law for both leaders and people, to help in bringing awareness in the country.

Undue Perks, Privileges and Benefits for Members of Parliament - will shock you.

A Government servant retiring in accordance with the Pension Rules is entitled to receive pension on completion of at least 10 years of qualifying service. Where is the justice in giving pension to MLA/MP for only 5 years...? MPs are entitled to a pension of Rs 25,000 per month after serving one term in Parliament and an increment of Rs 2,000 per month for every extra year of service thereafter. The salary of an MP has been fixed at Rs 1 lakh per month. MPs can avail 34 free domestic air journeys per year for themselves and their immediate families. They also get free first-class train travel for official and personal purposes and can claim mileage allowances for road travel within their constituencies.

The amount of daily allowance is Rs.2,000 (not taxable) for each day of residence on duty at a place where a session of a House of Parliament or a sitting of a Committee thereof is held. No member is liable to any proceedings in any court for anything said or any vote given by him/her in Parliament or its committees. Each MP is allowed to spend Rs. 2 crores in their constituency (who knows how much will go into their pocket?). For laundry service quarterly allowance of Rs. 75,000. A total of Rs 45,000 is entitled to each MP for office expenses. Out of these, Rs 15,000 is for meeting expenses on stationery items and postage, and Rs 30,000 is paid by the Lok Sabha/Rajya Sabha Secretariat to the person. Every member is entitled to three phones. MP can also have one mobile phone connection of MTNL and another mobile phone connection of MTNL/BSNL or any private mobile operator with national roaming facility. They can make 1,50,000 free local calls in a year. A free 3G net connection is also given. Guess the price of the food available in the canteen? A veg thali costs Rs 30 and a non veg thali costs Rs 90. Free medical care for immediate family members in select hospitals and all govt hospitals. Free water and 50,000 units of electricity per year.

CHAPTER IX

Environmental Issues

Major environmental issues in India are forests and agricultural degradation of land, resource depletion (such as water, mineral, forest, sand, and rocks), environmental degradation, soil- water-air-sound pollution, public health, deforestation with loss of biodiversity, loss of resilience in ecosystems, poor management of waste, growing water scarcity, falling groundwater tables, livelihood security for the poor, lake of awareness of environmental protection, burning waste and dangerous items just as plastic, rubber, tyres, etc. However, pollution (of air, soil, water, sound) still remains a major problem. Environmental issues are one of the primary causes of disease, health issues and long term livelihood impact for India.

Environmental degradation

Over 60% of India's arable land is estimated to suffer from environmental degradation. This has been caused both by a rapidly growing poor population seeking subsistence and by the misappropriation of natural resources by the wealthy for luxury consumption. Majority of poor people are directly dependent on natural resources for their basic needs like food, fodder fuel and shelter. Environment degradation has adversely affected the status of poor who depend upon natural resources for their immediate needs. Thus, the challenge of poverty and the challenge of environmental degradation are two sides of the same coin. The population growth and poverty are interlinked as every child is the breadwinner for the family.

Total land area of India is 329 million hectares out of which only 266 million hectares have potential productivity. 143 million hectares of land is under cultivation and the remaining land area

(85 million hectares) has suffered from soil degradation. Nearly 30% of the land in India is degraded. From 123 million hectares, 40 million hectare land is completely unproductive. Overgrazing, water and soil erosion leads to further land degradation. This degradation can be avoided by reforestation. There is a long history of study and debate about the interactions between population growth and the environment. A growing population exerts pressure on agricultural land, causing environmental degradation, and forcing the cultivation of land of higher as well as poorer quality. This environmental degradation ultimately reduces agricultural yields and food availability, famines and diseases and death.

Deforestation and Loss of biodiversity

The present forest cover in India (2023) is only 21.7% out the recommended 33% cover. Since the start of this century, India has lost 19% of its total tree cover. While 2.8% of forests were cut down. Forest cover forms a great carbon sink improving climate. Forests also play a vital role in enhancing the quality of environment by influencing the ecological balance and life support system (checking soil erosion, maintaining soil fertility, conserving water, regulating water cycle and floods, balancing carbon dioxide and oxygen content in atmosphere etc.) We are dependent on natural ecosystems for the products obtained from forests, grasslands, oceans and from agriculture and livestock as well as water, air, soil, minerals, oil etc. which are indispensable part of our life support systems. Life would be impossible without these substances. Increase in population puts pressure on these limited natural resources. Although deforestation is officially cited at 0.37 million acres/year, more sensitive estimates put it at 2.5 million acres/year. Deforestation and massive soil erosion have further created silting, flooding, and pollution in the plains areas of the country. In rural areas, poverty has become intertwined with resource degradation - poor soils, depleted aquifers and degraded forests. Destruction of forests leads to soil erosion, less rainfall, air impurity, higher temperature, loss of biodiversity and wildlife, etc. To subsist, the poor are compelled to mine and overuse these limited resources, creating a downward spiral of impoverishment and environmental degradation. There is growing pressure to better protect India's pockets of mega-biodiversity which are increasingly recognized as being of immense significance for global biodiversity, yet are increasingly threatened. Within the Indian four biodiversity hotspots, 25 species have become extinct in recent years.

Coastal Zone Management

India's 7,500km long coastal zone is endowed with fragile ecosystems including mangroves, coral reefs, estuaries, lagoons, and unique marine and terrestrial wildlife, which contribute in a significant manner to the national economy. Most of the coastal areas are polluted with plastic garbage, which enters the sea. Economic activities such as rapid urban-industrialization, maritime transport, marine fishing, tourism, coastal and seabed mining, offshore oil and natural gas production, aquaculture, and the recent setting up of special economic zones have led to a significant exploitation of these resources.In addition to the contribution of increased economic activity, coastal development and livelihoods are under stress due to pollution and climate change.

Pollution

The major sources of pollution in India include the rapid burning of fuelwood and biomass such as dried waste from livestock as the primary source of energy, lack of organised garbage and waste removal services, lack of sewage treatment operations, lack of flood control and monsoon water drainage system, diversion of consumer waste into rivers, using large land area for burial purposes, cremation practices near major rivers, government mandated protection of highly polluting old public transport, and continued operation by Indian government of government-owned, high emission plants built between 1950 and 1980. Reflecting the size of its economy and population, India is ranked as the sixth largest emitter of greenhouse gas emissions in the world.

Pollution of land and water has affected plants, animals and human beings. The quality of soil is deteriorating resulting in the loss of agricultural land. The loss is estimated to be about five to seven million hectares of land each year. Soil erosion, as a result of wind and/or water, costs the world dearly. The recurring floods have their own peculiar casualties like deforestation, silt in the river bed, inadequate and improper drainage, loss of men and property. The vast oceans, after being turned into dumping grounds for all nuclear wastes, have poisoned and polluted the whole natural environment. Two of the most important festivals cause pollution. On 'Bhogi Pongal' (harvest festival), all old waste garbage is gathered and burnt causing air pollution. On the festival of 'Fireworks" (Deepavali), air, soil and water get heavily polluted by the poisonous smoke, paper waste and poison chemicals from the unburst or improperly burnt firecrackers.

Air pollution

Undoubtedly, one of the most pressing environmental issues in India is air pollution. A Swiss IQ firm compiled a list of most polluted cities of the world and out of 50 world cities, an incredible 39 of those were in India. It also ranked India as the eighth most polluted nation in the world in 2022. According to the 2021 World Air Quality Report, India is home to 63 of the 100 most polluted cities of the world, with New Delhi named the capital with the worst air quality in the world. The study also found that PM2.5 concentrations – tiny particles in the air that are 2.5 micrometres or smaller in length – in 48% of the country's cities are more than 10 times higher than the 2021 WHO air quality guideline level. Vehicular emissions, industrial waste, smoke from cooking, the construction sector, crop burning, and power generation are among the biggest sources of air pollution in India. The country's dependence on coal, oil, and gas due to rampant electrification makes it the world's third-largest polluter, contributing over 2.65 billion metric tonnes of carbon to the atmosphere every year.

In 2021, India was among the world's most polluted countries, second only to Bangladesh. The annual average PM2.5 levels in India was about 58.1 µg/m³ in 2021, "ending a three-year trend of improving air quality" and a clear sign that the country has returned to pre-pandemic levels. Scientists have linked persistent exposure to PM2.5 to many long-term health issues including heart and lung disease, as well as 7 million premature deaths each year. A recent report published in Lancet Planetary Health states that 33,000 deaths in 10 cities in India every year can be attributed to air pollution levels that are below India's national clean air threshold. The authors used data on PM2.5 exposure in the 10 cities and the daily counts of mortality between 2008 and 2019. The 10 cities are - Ahmedabad, Bengaluru, Chennai, Delhi, Hyderabad, Kolkata, Mumbai, Pune, Shimla, and Varanasi. Delhi recorded the highest number of air pollution-related deaths in the study period - a staggering 11.5% i.e. 12,000 deaths each year. It has a large trail of mortality due to largely respiratory infections—lung diseases, COPD, asthma bronchial infections. And it also leads to cardiac arrest and gastrointestinal problems. In November 2021, air pollution reached such severe levels that they were forced to shut down schools and several large power plants around Delhi. Out of the 15 most polluted places in the world, 10 cities are in North India alone (World air quality Report 2021). Automobile exhaust is the major source of pollution. It is estimated that two/three wheelers constitute about 75 percent of the total vehicles and cause more than 50 percent of the total vehicular pollution load.

Soil pollution

Soil pollution is defined as the presence of toxic chemicals (pollutants or contaminants) in the soil, in very high concentrations to pose a risk to human health and the ecosystem.

Soil pollution affects soil fertility; this jeopardises food security, which is essential for human survival. It also poses risks to human health — both indirectly through the consumption of contaminated food and drinking water, and directly through exposure to contaminated soil. According to the National Bureau of Soil Survey and Land Use Planning, around 30% of the soil in India is degraded. Of this, around 29% is lost to the sea, 61% is transferred from one place to another, and 10% is deposited in reservoirs.

Soil degradation is due to man-made factors like mining, deforestation, overgrazing, monoculture farming, excessive tillage, and the use of chemical fertilisers and pesticides. Soil can be contaminated from industrial activity, chemical and petroleum spills, fertilisers and pesticides used in farming, landfills and fires. The consequences of humans ingesting such pollutants can include lead poisoning, deteriorating health, allergies and reduced immune system strength. The pesticide residues were detected in 4,510 samples (19.1%). The maximum number of residues were detected in the samples of vegetables, fruits and spices. Out of 4,510 samples with detection, the residues in 523 (2.22%) samples were found exceeding Food Safety and Standards Authority of India's 'Maximum Residue Limit' (MRL) as given in its website-fssai.gov.in. India is the largest producer and user of pesticides, too. Overusing pesticides has destroyed millions of hectares of soil in India. Soil pollution can negatively affect the metabolisms of microorganisms and arthropods, destroying some levels of the food chain and negatively affecting predators. Smaller life forms ingest the harmful chemicals in the soil, which then pass up the food chain to larger animals, leading to increased mortality rates and even extinction.

Another serious issue of soil pollution is due to dumping garbage, plastics wastes and other solid waste; disposal of electrical items such as batteries causes an adverse effect on the soil due to the presence of harmful chemicals. Eg: lithium present in batteries can cause the leaching of soil. Human waste such as urine, faeces, diapers, etc is dumped directly in the land. It causes both soil and water pollution.Diseases caused by soil pollution include Irritation of the skin and the eyes, Headaches, nausea, vomiting, Coughing, pain in the chest, and wheezing.

Pollution can increase the salinity of the soil, making it barren and unsuitable for growing most types of plants. Any crops that manage to grow in such conditions would be toxic enough to cause health problems if eaten. There are about six million hectares of salty land in India. Every year, around 6,000-8,000 hectares of farmland in Punjab become unsuitable for cultivation. Remember that soil is a finite and irreplaceable resource that sustains life on Earth.

Solid waste pollution

Among the most pressing environmental issues in India is also waste. Indian cities alone generate more than 100 million tons of solid waste a year. Street corners are piled with trash. Public places and sidewalks are despoiled with filth and litter, rivers and canals act as garbage dumps. These invite all germs and flies spreading diseases. Medical waste is improperly disposed of. Unlike in the west, organised and segregated waste collection and processing is poor in India. Improper collection, transportation, treatment and disposal of solid wastes have resulted in increased pollution and health hazard from these wastes. Urban Municipal Wastes (MSW) is a heterogeneous mixture of paper, plastic, cloth, metal, glass, organic matter etc. generated from households, commercial establishments and markets.

As the largest population in the world of nearly 1.4 billion people (2022), it comes as no surprise that 277 million tonnes of municipal solid waste (MSW) are produced there every year. Experts estimate that by 2030, MSW is likely to reach 387.8 million tonnes and will more than double the current value by 2050. India's rapid urbanisation makes waste management extremely challenging. Currently, about 5% of the total collected waste is recycled, 18% is composted, and the remaining is dumped at landfill sites. Without appropriate sewerage and sanitation facilities, the accumulated wastes could mix with open-water resources, leading to high levels of water pollution. Fly Ash, phospho-gypsum and iron & steel slags are the main forms of industrial solid wastes generated in India. Besides, around 5 million tonnes of hazardous wastes is generated annually with very little infrastructure for proper disposal of these wastes. The effects of mixing agricultural runoff containing wastes, pesticides, and fertilisers, in the rural water-sources, would also need consideration.

Water pollution

Besides its air, the country's waterways have become extremely polluted, with around 70% of surface water estimated to be unfit for consumption. Illegal dumping of raw sewage, silt, and garbage into rivers and lakes severely contaminated India's waters. The near-total absence of pipe planning and an inadequate waste management system are only exacerbating the situation. Every day, a staggering 40 million litres of wastewater enter rivers and other water bodies. Of these, only a tiny fraction is adequately treated due to a lack of adequate infrastructure. Leaching chemical fertilisers and pesticides, industrial effluents have polluted surface water and affected the quality of the groundwater. It is essential to maintain the water quality of rivers and other water bodies.

Strategies for provision of safe drinking water and keeping water bodies clean are the key challenges. According to the World Bank, roughly 163 million Indians lack access to safe drinking water, 210 million Indians lack access to improved sanitation, 21% of communicable diseases are linked to unsafe water and 500 children under the age of five die from diarrhoea each day in India. Besides affecting humans, with nearly 40 million Indians suffering from waterborne diseases like typhoid, cholera, and hepatitis and nearly 400,000 fatalities each year, water pollution also damages crops, as infectious bacteria and diseases in the water used for irrigation prevent them from growing. More than half of the rivers in India are highly polluted with numerous others at levels considered unsafe by modern standards. The waters of the Yamuna, Ganga and Sabarmati flow the dirtiest with a deadly mix of pollutants, both hazardous and organic. The Ganges is considered to be HOLY and is the fifth most polluted river in the world. It contains human waste and industrial contaminants, but provides water for about 40% of India's population, yet millions of Indians depend on it for their daily needs.

About 400 rivers enter the sea along the 7,500 km coastline in India. Out of the world's 1000 most polluted rivers, 144 are in India that end in oceans along coastline. These most polluted 1000 rivers of the world account for 80% of global annual emissions, which range between 0.8 million and 2.7 million metric tons per year. A number of chemicals, petrochemical and other industries in the coastal areas have resulted in significant discharge of industrial effluents into the coastal water bodies. Heavy metals such as lead and cadmium were found in Thane creek off Mumbai coast. The Cochin region of Kerala coast has been found affected by petroleum hydrocarbons. Coral reefs which are very productive marine ecosystem are adversely affected.

Plastic pollution

The plastic crisis in India is one of the worst on the planet. According to the Central Pollution Control Board (CPCB), India currently produces more than 25,000 tonnes of plastic waste every day on average, which accounts for almost 6% of the total solid waste generated in the country. India stands second among the top 20 countries having a high proportion of riverine plastic emissions nationally as well as globally. Indus, Brahmaputra, and Ganges rivers are known as the 'highways of plastic flows' as they carry and drain most of the plastic debris in the country. Together with the 10 other topmost polluted rivers, they leak nearly 90% of plastics into the sea globally.

Plastic waste pollution, a global crisis requiring urgent action, especially in oceans and rivers, is an emerging environmental hazard and accumulation on riverbanks, deltas, coastlines, and the ocean surface is rapidly increasing. Of all the plastics ever made to date, it was estimated that 60% has been discarded in landfills or in the natural environment. Plastic pollution poses threats on aquatic life, ecosystems, and human health. Plastic litter also causes severe economic losses through damage to vessels and fishing gear, negative effects on the tourism industry, and increased shoreline cleaning efforts. Work on the origin and fate of plastic pollution in aquatic environments suggests that land-based plastics are one of the main sources of marine plastic pollution, either by direct emission from coastal zones or by transport through rivers. Rivers are a major source of plastic waste in the oceans. Trillions of pieces of plastic pollute our oceans today, and the problem is worsening. This plastic has a devastating impact on marine wildlife and ecosystems. Plastics can persist for many decades, continuously degrading into microplastics. These can be ingested by wildlife and later enter the human food chain.

Noise Pollution

This is another important pollution in India. Excessive noise that may harm the activity or balance of human or animal life. The source of most outdoor noise is mainly caused by transportation systems, constant unnecessary honking by two or three wheelers, buses, trucks, motor vehicles, aircraft, trains, diesel generators, construction work, loud speakers (from mosques with 4 to 6 loudspeakers, temples, meetings) and loud fireworks bursting at any time.The indiscriminate use of loudspeakers (with high volume) for political meetings and for songs or sermons in temples and mosques (5 'azan' prayer calls from 4.30 to 8.30 PM) make noise pollution in residential areas worse. From both religious and practical point of views, there is no justification for using loudspeakers at mosques for azan recitals with maximum volume. It disturbs the early morning sleep for the sick and elderly like me. Even many Islamic nations such as Saudi Arabia, Indonesia have restricted the volume to one third of the maximum due to complaints of disturbance. Will India do the same? Festivals, weddings, and religious events often involve the use of loudspeakers and firecrackers, contributing to elevated noise levels. Even inside churches or indoor wedding functions, high volume is used. Studies by Central Pollution Control Board (CPCB), on the ambient noise levels show that noise levels in most of the big cities exceed the prescribed standards. There is no enforcement of use or noise level regulations. High noise levels can contribute to Tinnitus, hearing loss, irritability, cardiovascular effects in humans and an increased incidence of coronary artery disease.

Environmental awareness

In India, environmental awareness gained importance in the 1970s after the UN sponsored conference on environment in Stockholm (1972). The Indian government undertook many environmentally friendly activities. The Ministry of environment and forest was established and laws were enacted on environment protection in 1986. Environment awareness is very high in western nations where even a small kid does not throw waste paper or cover on the road or anywhere or even in a forest. Just the opposite here in India, no one, young or old, don't have any awareness.

CHAPTER X

Socio-Religious Issues

Hinduism is often regarded as the oldest surviving religion in the world, with roots tracing back to prehistoric times, over 5,000 years ago. Hinduism spread to Nepal, Ceylon, parts of Southeastern Asia, China and other neighbouring nations. Buddhism is an offshoot of Hinduism; Siddhartha Gautama (563 or 483 BC), a royal prince of Kapilavastu (Nepal), saw sick suffering and death, was shaken, left his family in Palace and went to meditate under a Banyan tree (Ficus religiosa) in a forest. After attaining 'enlightenment', he found that Desire is the cause for all Evil in this world. So became known as 'Lord Buddha' , that is 'the enlightened one'. After originating in India, Buddhism spread throughout Central Asia, Sri Lanka, Tibet, Southeast Asia, as well as the East Asian countries of China, Mongolia, Korea, Japan and Vietnam. Jainism and Sikhism were born out of Hinduism and include in their ideas a rejection of the Vedas, the main scriptures of the Hindu faith. Jainism was founded in Rajasthan by Mahavira (599-527 BC) called Jina (Spiritual Conqueror). The Jains believe that there is no real god. Guru Nanak founded Sikhism in Punjab in the late 15th century based on universal love. Christianity was introduced by the arrival of Saint Thomas, a disciple of Jesus, as early as 52 AD. Islam entered with the invasion of Arabs (?traders) and Mughal kings in 712 AD..

When Aryans invaded India in the Vedic period, 1800-1500 BC, they saw to it that their religious beliefs and ideologies have the upperhand over the conquered races in India. The prevalent myths were so re-interpreted or imposed that the Aryan gods were always supreme and victorious. Their female goddesses were subordinated to other existing male gods, thus making the matriarchal system subordinate to the patriarchal system. The oppressive caste system also was introduced to make Aryans a superior race to local Dravidians. So the Brahmins (Aryans), the uppermost caste, became the sole authorities on religious scriptures, its study and interpretation and only they can become priests of temples. The lowest caste, 'Shudras' were debarred from it and were made subservient to higher castes. This anti cultural seed sown by them has borne fruit a hundredfold resulting in the immiserisation of people who can hardly be called 'human beings'. These outcasts (Shudras) were called Untouchables, as they performed the least desirable activities and jobs, such as dealing with dead bodies, cleaning toilets and washrooms, and tanning and dyeing leather. Even the theory of rebirth may be an invention to legitimise the oppressive caste culture. The composition of religions are as follows:-

Hinduism (79.8%)
Islam (14.2%)
Christianity (2.3%)
Sikhism (1.7%)
Buddhism (0.7%)
Adivasi (0.5%)
Jainism (0.4%)
Atheism/Agnostic (0.25%)

Religious Intolerance

The Indian Constitution guarantees freedom of religion, which has led to a harmonious relationship between the different religions practised in India. But, in recent years under the ruling Bharatiya Janata Party (BJP), led by Prime Minister Narendra Modi, the BJP is often described as promoting a Hindu nationalist ideology, especially in elections (playing the communal card). They project themselves as 'Protector of Hinduism' to gain votes as Hindus form the majority. The BJP's appeal is great among Hindus. As the famous satirist and writer Kushwant Singh said, "*the absolute corruption of religion that has made us among the most brutal people on earth*". Religion is not the only fault line in Indian society. In some regions of the country, significant shares of people perceive widespread, caste-based discrimination. Out of 28 states, 10 states have passed Anti-Conversion laws.

The U.S. Commission on International Religious Freedom (USCIRF) has recommended that India, along with Afghanistan, Syria, Nigeria and Vietnam, be added to the U.S. government's list of Countries of Particular Concern, or CPC, because of the worsening limits on religious freedom in these countries. Religious intolerance in India was called 'Frightening'. The advocacy group Open Doors ranks India 11th on its 2023 World Watch List, saying that it is, in parts, "a scary place to be a Christian."

According to Delhi-based groups, the United Christian Forum had at the end of 2023 stated on average, two Christians face attacks daily in India. This report was released on December 14, revealing a staggering total of 687 reported incidents of violence against Christians within the span of 334 days in 2023. During the last 10 years saw an increase in attacks on churches and Christians. 'Hindu extremists (Bajrang Dal, RSS, and VHP-Vishwa Hindu Parishad) come to churches or Christian schools wielding lathis, accompanied by a local photographer and often by the police. They disrupt the prayer service, beat up the pastor, and if it is in a building, they attack the building, desecrate the Bible, break statutes, loot offerings, etc., says Activist John Dayal'. Hindu nationalists have frequently and falsely accused Christians of forced conversion under duress and have used these claims as a pretext for violence. Chhattisgarh, UP., Haryana states have most cases of violence against Christians

Recently, racial violence (incited by Political system) in the Indian state of Manipur has left more than 60 people dead, thousands displaced, and burned-out churches smouldering. While the clashes pitted a largely Hindu ethnic group against a chiefly Christian one, The dispute does not appear to be driven principally by religious differences."what began as an inter-ethnic clash hastily developed an inter-religious dimension" due to the polarised atmosphere created by what he called "the majoritarian Hindutva regime at the national level." Following two incidents will speak for themselves...

The most gruesome attack that shocked the whole world, took place in Orissa in 1999. Graham Stuart Staines, an Australian missionary worker and his two young sons aged only 6 and 10 were burned to death when the vehicle in which they were sleeping was set fire at night by extremist group Bajrang Dal. He has been helping the poor tribals and lepers since 1965.

In Jhabua, Madhya Pradesh in 1998 around 18-26 men barged their way into the Medical centre with Ashram in where the nuns lived and ransacked the entire ashram and some of the men gang raped the nuns. Similarly, in 2015, six extremists ransacked the convent school in Ranaghat (West Bengal) and stole money before entering the convent itself and gang raped a 73 old sister. They also stole money from the school, he said, vandalised the chapel, broke open the tabernacle and took away the ciborium, the sacred vessel used during Mass. One Bangladeshi muslim was convicted for the rape and attempted murder.

Fr. Stan Swamy (83 yrs), a Jesuit priest in Jharkhand who worked for the upliftment and rights of tribals/adivasis, was arrested by the NIA in 2020, from Bagaicha, a Jesuit social action centre, and charged under the Unlawful Activities (Prevention) Act. The Jesuits denied the allegation of Swamy being a Maoist, by stating that it was against the ethos of the Jesuit order. Swamy's requests for bail were repeatedly denied, despite his deteriorating health. Swamy, who suffered from Parkinson's Disease, reportedly became unable to feed and bathe himself. Prison authorities also reportedly denied him basic amenities, such as a straw and sipper, to help with his Parkinson's. He was almost tortured in jail and died, due to Covid in 2021 under custody. In 2022, the UN Working Group on Arbitrary Detention released an opinion, declaring Swamy's detention arbitrary and his death "utterly preventable."

Socio-Religious factors

India is a highly religious nation, the home to four great religions as mentioned earlier. In Hinduism, social life is intrinsically connected with religious life. In rural India, religious ideas and values dominate over economic and political values. Social obligations are religiously sanctioned. But India is also a country where religion has been a barrier to human and nations progress. Like Hinduism being one of the oldest religions of the world, so too the Hindu religious philosophy is one of the ancient philosophies. Hindus believe in the doctrines of 'samsara' (continuous cycle of life, death and reincarnation), and 'karma' (universal law of cause and effect). This philosophy holds that living creatures have a soul, transmigration of souls and they're all part of the supreme soul. Its scriptures are a compendium of high theology on man, god, universe and nature.

But the religion followed by the common Hindu has very little to do with these philosophical and theological beliefs. Their daily life runs on do's and don'ts laid by tradition and society. There is no central authority to correct or question any one's religious belief, one follows his own conscience as it has been formed by the society. Unfortunately, the doyens of spiritual learning have not evolved a meaningful and liberating the Hindu theology. Due to the illiteracy of the people, very often superstitions guide them. Some of the old cultural and socio-religious evils like 'Sati', Devadasi system and child marriage have mostly gone.

Caste and Karma

The oppressive caste system was introduced by the invaded Aryan race to make them a superior race to local Dravidians. So the Brahmins (Aryans), the uppermost caste, became the sole authorities on religious scriptures, its study and interpretation and only they can become priests of temples. Probably the Aryans had only three social classes, the warriors, priests and common people. After invasion by around 1000 BC, they developed four main caste distinctions: Brahamin, consisting of priests, scholars, and teachers;

Kshatriyas, the kings, governors, and warriors; Vaishyas, comprising agriculturists, artisans, and merchants; and Sudras, the service providers and artisans. The conquered native dark skinned Dravidians were called 'shudras', lowest class as they were entirely of different race or stock.

According to their laws, a Brahmin enjoyed the highest status in society as he was the chief mediator between God and man (like a prophet in Christian religion). He should not do hard work (4:2-7), Gifts to a brahmin strongly recommended (3:98). When a king conquers a new area, he should not take away the property of brahmins. While a shudra should always serve others. Serving the brahmin forms the highest duty of a shudra's life (10:123) and God created a shudra to do servile work for brahmins. If he performs these duties, he can attain a higher caste in his rebirth to next life. A shudra is a property of the brahmin, he cannot learn vedas or cannot accumulate wealth. By their very birth, these shudras are outcastes and untouchables (Dalits) and must live totally segregated from other castes, outside the village. Dalits are not allowed to enter a temple or wear shoes; if they wear them, Dalits will have to take off their shoes at times when they meet a higher caste person. They should not sit at bus stops or in the bus, even if seats are vacant. Even the great poet Thulasidas wrote that 'shudras come only after dogs!' The cows are considered more sacred than them! Even now, more than 160 million lower-caste "untouchables" in India live in sub-human conditions and face increasing discrimination, violence, rape and murder, according to the World Human Rights Watch. There are 200 million Dalits in India out of a population of 1.3 billion. Mass conversions of lower caste Hindus to Christianity and Islam took place in order to escape the discrimination. Though untouchability was abolished legally in 1950, in reality it remains embedded in India's psyche.

Nearly 90 per cent of the country's billionaire wealth has been found concentrated in the hands of the upper castes who hold nearly 55 per cent of the national wealth, according to the All-India Debt and Investment Survey (AIDIS) for 2018-19. This stark contrast in wealth ownership underscores the deep-seated economic inequalities rooted in India's caste system.

The doctrine of 'karma': Close on the heels of the caste system is the doctrine of karma that further enables the caste inequalities to be rooted in the social system of Hinduism. One is born shudra because of his previous evil life. This is karma. Thus the caste system and doctrine of karma are interrelated and no one dares to challenge this system.

Superstitious beliefs in India

Superstition is defined as any belief or practice that is based on supernatural occurrences and contradicts modern science or reasoning. Superstition in India is considered a widespread social problem. This belief has also hindered the advancement of India. Superstitions are usually attributed to lack of education; however, this has not always been the case in India, as there are many educated people with beliefs considered superstitious by the public.Though many of the ridiculous beliefs have gone, even at present some of the superstitions exist especially among the rural illiterate, literate conservative or religious Hindus. Many educated people have also been observed following beliefs that may be considered superstitious. The beliefs and practices vary from region to region, with many states or regions having their own specific beliefs.

'Even though India has faced many changes and development in the field of science and technology, the belief of the people over superstitions still exists in the Society'. Sethi and Sain (2019) did a study on prevalence of superstitions to find out whether superstitious beliefs still play a crucial role in the belief pattern of educated and uneducated females and to find out to what extent it affects their lives. Many superstitious beliefs have been in Indian society for such a long time that they have become a habit. Superstitions have led to the carrying out of Human sacrifices, Witch-hunting, abuses and misuse by godmen and faith healers.

Common superstitions in India today include a black cat crossing the road being bad luck, cutting fingernails/toenails at night being bad luck, a crow calling meaning that guests are arriving, drinking milk after eating fish causing skin diseases, and itchy palms signalling the arrival of money. Few of the superstitions followed are given below:-

Eclipses are bad omens for pregnant women

Pregnant women in India have a hard time during eclipses. Not only are they supposed to stay indoors during the entire time, they're not even allowed to sit cross-legged. God forbid the baby should be born with ugly marks all over its body.

An itchy left palm means money is coming to you

Been wanting to escape to an exotic holiday location? Have an eye on that swanky new car? All you've got to do is close your eyes and wish really really hard that your left palm starts to itch soon!

Lemon and chillies can ward off evil

As long as you hang a string of seven chillies and a lemon outside your home, no evil will dare approach you. This charm also applies to one's place of work. According to a Hindu legend, Alakshmi, the goddess of misfortune, likes sour and spicy food. So she satisfies her hunger with the lemon and chillies and returns content without ever stepping inside the house and bringing in a trail of bad luck.

If a black cat crosses your path, it's a bad omen

Just because they are black cats? Not just in India but this is a popular belief in the west too. The origin of this superstition has come from the Egyptians who believed that black cats were evil creatures and they bring bad luck. In India, black colour is generally associated with the Lord Shani. It is said that if a black cat crosses your path, then you should let somebody else pass before you do. This way, the first person will have all the bad luck and you won't.

Human Sacrifice to appease spirits or get treasure

Although human sacrifices are not prevalent in India, rare isolated incidents do happen, especially in rural areas. In some cases, humans have been replaced by animals like goats. It is alleged that cases often go unreported or are covered up. Between 1999 and

2006, about 200 cases of child sacrifices were reported from Uttar Pradesh state in North India.

Good and Bad days

In Hinduism, people are believed to have auspicious or favourable days on which they will have a high probability of success in any task they do. Such days with a certain time are calculated based on the individual's birth star, moon, and planetary phases. Starting a business or businesses signing new deals or starting new ventures is mostly conducted on auspicious days. Hindu marriages are also fixed in matching auspicious time and date of a bride and groom according to their Horoscope. If the horoscope of the bride and groom don't match, then no marriage.

The new moon day in the Hindu lunar calendar, holds immense significance in astrology and spirituality. The time of the new moon is not generally favourable for celebrations, significant activities, or new beginnings. Usually Hindus fast on that day. People should avoid performing any auspicious activity like buying a new dress, vehicle or anything new. The new moon has many beliefs concerning it. Full moon day is considered to bring good luck. There is another joke...relating Science and superstition; when the Space research chief of Moon landing project as Hindu astrologer about the auspicious day to shoot spacecraft to Moon, the astrologer suggested a Full moon day and not to send therocket on New moon day as Moon 'disappears'!

Solar and lunar eclipses

Several superstitions exist with eclipses.Solar eclipses are associated with war, violent events and disasters. People don't eat or cook food during the event and Temples are closed before the event and reopened after the event is over. Pregnant women are advised to stay indoors. It is considered inauspicious to give birth during the event. Similar beliefs exist for lunar eclipse too.

Godmen and Fortune tellers (Palmistry)

The word godman in modern usage is a colloquial blanket term used for charismatic spiritual leaders in India claiming to have healing, psychic and magic powers. Some of them have built large pan-

Indian or international networks as they charge hefty high fees for their 'darshan' (blessing). They usually have a high-profile presence with high political connections, and are capable of attracting attention and support from large sections of the society. Despite many gurus and babas implicated for crimes including murder, rape, tax evasion and fraud, Indians continue to flock to self-styled godmen. Even though such godmen were implicated for crimes like murder, rape, tax evasion and fraud, people's unhealthy obsession with these babas continues.

Theerthapada, also known as Sree Hari, has preached at several temples in Kerala and was revered by hundreds of Hindu families in the state. He was recently charged with rape; he now joins the long and dubious list of several self-styled gurus presently languishing in various prisons nationwide for numerous sexual assault offences.

Three years ago, police had to battle the supporters of Rampal Singh Jatin, a controversial guru from the northern state of Haryana before they could arrest him. Their investigations uncovered sordid details about the supposedly holy man's sex life - a world of abuse, rape, murder and excess that was just as remarkable as his sprawling abode. He preferred "hostesses," whom he called "sadhikayaen" and during the raids police recovered pregnancy kits from Rampal's room, besides sexual potency drugs.

Another self-styled spiritual godman of Gujarat, Asaram Bapu, was arrested in 2013 after a teenage girl accused him of rape. She claimed that the guru lured her by promising to cleanse her of evil spirits.

In 2010, controversial Hindu godman Swami Nityananda (in south) came under scanner after a leaked video showed him engaging in sexual activities with an actress from southern India and many other complaints molesting or raping several others. Cases were also filed in the USA and France. But when arrest warrants were issued in many states, he disappeared in 2019 and fled the country; still not traced.

Fortune telling is also common practice and they claim to predict the future by palm reading, parrot astrology, numerology and horoscope.

"People everywhere in India are prone to mystics. Many fall prey to the saffron robes these godmen wear believing they are true saviours, and afterwards blind faith takes over," stated Pradeep Singh, a sociologist. Despite the scandals and the fall from grace, there is no dearth of self-styled godmen operating in the country. Faith in the unreasonable and irrational remains firm.

Black Magic and Witchcraft

Some people, mostly in villages, have the belief that witchcraft and black magic are effective and some seek advice from witch doctors for health, financial or marital problems. According to reports, widows or divorcees tend to be targeted to rob them of their property. NCW (National Commission for women) in 2015 reported that 768 women had been murdered for allegedly practising witchcraft since 2008. And between 2001 and 2006, an estimated 300 people branded as witches or black magicians, were killed in the state of Assam

'Vastu'

'Vastu' defines how a house or a building should be constructed and how the orientation and direction and location of rooms and doors should be arranged. Many construction companies in India construct buildings according to it. This is similar to 'Feng Shui' in China, but with more psychological implications for not following 'vastu' rules. Hindus believe that bad things happen in their life or deterioration of their health or disputes or division in family arise if proper 'vastu' is not followed in house construction.

CHAPTER XI

Conclusion

Kushwant Singh (2003) in his epic book 'End of India' summarised as follows: "I thought the nation was coming to an end,' wrote Khushwant Singh, looking back on the violence of Partition that he witnessed over half a century ago. He believed then that he had seen the worst that India could do to herself. But after the violence in Gujarat in 2002, he had reason to feel that the worst, perhaps, is still to come. Analysing the communal violence in Gujarat in 2002, the anti-Sikh riots of 1984, the burning of Graham Staines and his children, the targeted killings by terrorists in Punjab and Kashmir, Khushwant Singh forces us to confront the absolute corruption of religion that has made us among the most brutal people on earth. He also points out that fundamentalism has less to do with religion than with politics. And communal politics, he reminds us, is only the most visible of the demons we have nurtured and let loose upon ourselves".

The book 'A Nation of Idiots' (2019) says, "We Indians are an Interesting bunch! Intolerant to the debate on intolerance, but tolerant of religious intolerance. We cling onto age-old traditions, but a holiday can alter our accent. To us, caste and community is a badge of trust, religion is a line of control and a godman is an anti-depressant. We won't stop at a zebra crossing, but we will damn well stop on it. We build things to prove our worth and break things to prove a point. We love the concept of independence, but we need our parents to help raise our kids. And we scripted the Kamasutra. Easy to forget, since we also ruined sex. So how do we tell the real from the farcical? The farcical from the nutty? And the nutty from the downright ridiculous? Easy. We just go along", states Daksh Tyagi (2019) in his book 'A Nation of Idiots'.

In conclusion, thus the roots of degeneration had their birth many centuries back. As a person who values honesty, discipline, punctuality and other virtues, my own observations and experiences in life in this nation have caused frustration and sadness. This prompted me to write this book. As compared to the numerous parks, long trails for safe walking and green spaces in every community in the west, green spaces and parks for spending leisure time, especially for kids and elderly, are lacking here. Most of the places, road side pavements are absent for safe walking. I feel daily most irritated by noise pollution, especially unnecessary honking, flies from roadside garbage disturbing my walk on the roadside, with constant fear of accidents. I have been chased and once bitten by a street dog. As in the West, there are no roadside pavements for safe walking. (Even now, frequently street dogs don't like me walking on their street and bark at me) I have been in accidents while driving my bike when the other person did not follow the rule while turning. In 2018, I consulted Allergy specialist Dr V.Anand for my allergy problems. I underwent allergy tests and found my respiratory allergies were due to dust, humidity and polluted air. He said that India is a country that is unfit for me to live. If I want relief, I have to emigrate or go to a place with a dust free, pure atmosphere. If given an opportunity, I will gladly emigrate to the west where air is pure, plenty of green spaces and absence of honking.

The average Indian attitude is 'Who bothers rules and regulations?' Another visible nature is 'utter selfishness' in public places, not bothered about inconvenience to others. They offer so much cash or gold to Gods in temples, but are not ready to help the poor, needy and downtrodden or feed the hungry. There may be exceptions. Life is very comfortable for those upperclass folk with power and money, but for the majority poor or downtrodden. The rich become evil because of their wealth and power, while the poor are forced into evil ways by their sheer necessity. Surely India needs a revolution, one that basically changes from indiscipline, selfish nature, laziness, cheating, injustice, inequality to foster values of love, brotherhood, tolerance, justice, discipline, hard working, equality, honesty, integrity,

CHAPTER XII

References Cited

Anang Pal Malik (2016) 'Corruption in India', Locksley Hall Publishing. India.

Balarajan Y, Selvaraj S, Subramanian SV. Health care and equity in India. Lancet. 2011;377:505–15.

Daksh Tyagi (2019) 'A Nation of Idiots' Every Protest Publications. India.

Edward Oliveira. (1983) 'Factors responsible for the present pathetic Indian situation'. Thesis submitted for B.Th,, Jnana Deepa Vidyapeeth, Pune (unpublished). Pp 63.

Forster E.M. (1924) 'A Passage to India'. Diamond Pocket Books Pvt Ltd (1940 Edition), Pp.338.

Gulshan Kumar (2021) 'A Study on Corruption in India.' International Journal of Social Science and Humanities Research. 9:4, 237-242.

Gurleen Kaur Sethi & Navreet Kaur Sain (2019) 'Prevalence of Superstitions in Indian Society in the 21st Century'. International Journal of Nursing Education, Vol.11, No. 4: pages 56-60.

Kushwant Singh (2015) 'Gods and Godmen of India'. Harper Collins India. Pp 248.

Kushwant Singh (2003) 'End of India', Penguin books India. Pp.173.

Mukesh Eashwaran (1997) 'Why Poverty Persists in India: A Framework for Understanding the Indian Economy', Oxford University press.

Mysha Momtaz, Saniya Yesmin Bubli & Mohidus Samad Khan (2023) *Mechanisms and Health Aspects of Food Adulteration: A Comprehensive Review." Foods. 2023 Jan; 12(1): 199.

Ramasamy,B. (2013) 'Scheduled Castes-Harijan in India.' Daya Publishing house India.

Senthilkumar, D. 2021. 'The less sparkled dark side of India: Why India is at the back?'. Notion Press, Chennai, Pp.24.

Sethi J.D. (1975) 'Indian in Crisis'. Vikas Publications, New Delhi. p77.

Umesh Upadhyay (2024) 'Western media narratives on India: From Gandhi to Modi', Rupa publications (India) Ltd. pp184.

Balarajan Y, Selvaraj S, Subramanian SV. Health care and equity in India. Lancet. 2011;377:505–15.

Appendix- Previous books by the author published by Notion Press:-

1. Food is Medicine - 2020
2. Plants as medicine - 2020
3. Live a healthy 100 - 2021
4. Seven laws of success in Life - 2022
5. Why Humanity is unable to solve its Problems? -2022
6. Discovering the Real JESUS - 2022
7. Three greatest Saints & their greatest Miracles - 2023
8. Creation or Evolution? - 2023
9. Crossover - 2024.